This book belongs to a superhero called

....

To my own little superheroes . . . Rohan, Sajjan, Serena, Amrin, Oscar and Olivia – R.S.

For Anouska – L.D.

HODDER CHILDREN'S BOOKS
First published in Great Britain in 2020
by Hodder and Stoughton

10 9 8 7 6 5 4 3 2 1

Text © Ranj Singh, 2020
Illustrations © Hachette Children's Group, 2020
Illustrated by Liam Darcy

A CIP catalogue record for this book is available from the British Library.

ISBN 978 1 44495 900 0

Printed and bound in China

MIX
Paper from
responsible sources
FSC® C104740
www.fsc.org

HODDER CHILDREN'S BOOKS
An imprint of Hachette Children's Group
Part of Hodder and Stoughton
Carmelite House, 50 Victoria Embankment,
London EC4Y 0DZ

An Hachette UK Company
www.hachette.co.uk
www.hachettechildrens.co.uk

A SUPERHERO Like You

Dr Ranj

Illustrated by Liam Darcy

Hodder
Children's
Books

One morning, Lily woke up with a very **BIG** idea.

She knew she had to tell someone straight away.

Mum was getting ready for work.

"Guess what, Mummy?" said Lily. "I know what I'm going to do when I grow up. I'm going to be a **SUPERHERO!**"

"A superhero?" smiled Mum. "Like Captain Splat and Supersock?"

"No, Mummy," laughed Lily, "I'm not going to be one of those *silly* superheroes. I don't want to climb up the side of a building or wear my pants outside my trousers! I want to be a **REAL** superhero – the kind that helps people and makes the world a better place."

"That's a great idea," said Mum. "And what will you do when you're a **REAL** grown-up superhero?"

"Oh, there are **SO** many things I could do!" said Lily. "Maybe I'll be a **DOCTOR.** When someone feels poorly, I'll use my **SUPER** caring skills to make them all better."

"I think you'd be very good at that, Lily," said Mum.

"Or I could be a **FIREFIGHTER!**
If there's trouble in town, I'll race to the
rescue in my speedy red fire engine. When
I sound my super-siren, **EVERYONE** will
know that help is on the way."

"Perhaps I'll be a **TEACHER.**
My classroom will be full of fun!

Mars

Sun

Neptune

Together we can
explore space,
make art . . .

meet creepy-crawlies
and travel all over the world!"

"It would be **AMAZING** to fly an **AIR AMBULANCE!**
When someone is hurt, I'll be the first on the scene.

I'll fly through the clouds, high above the world,
bringing help to wherever it's needed."

"Or I could be a **CARER.** I'll meet amazing people and treat them all with kindness and love.

We'll share memories and make new ones together:

dancing . . .

laughing . . .

and telling
stories."

"Maybe I'll be a **RECYCLING-TRUCK DRIVER.**

I'll steer my **SUPER-COOL** truck down the city streets, collecting old things to make into new, just like magic. I'll help look after our amazing planet – and I'll help my neighbours too!"

"But what if I were a super **SCIENTIST?**
Just imagine the incredible things I could do! I'll make
amazing discoveries in my lab – I'll even make new
medicines to help people who are sick."

"Or maybe I'll be a **VET.** I'll look after poorly puppies and grumpy guinea pigs until they feel better.

With gentle care and lots of love, I'll help
get them back on their paws in no time!"

"You see, Mummy?" said Lily. "There are **SO** many ways that I can be a superhero. I know I'm small, but my superpowers of kindness, care and love are **BIG**, and I'm going to use them to make the world a better place.

When I grow up, **THAT'S** what I'm going to do.
I'm going to be a superhero, Mummy . . .

... just like

YOU."